FREDDIE

FLOSSIE

The BOBBSEY TWINS®

THE MYSTERY OF THE DINOSAUR IN THE FOREST

By **Laura Lee Hope**

Illustrated by Larry Ruppert

Little Simon
New York London Toronto Sydney

NAN

BERT

LITTLE SIMON

An imprint of Simon & Schuster Children's Publishing Division
1230 Avenue of the Americas, New York, New York 10020
Copyright © 2005 by Simon & Schuster, Inc.
All rights reserved, including the right of reproduction in whole or in part in any form.
LITTLE SIMON is a registered trademark of Simon & Schuster, Inc., and associated
colophon is a trademark of Simon & Schuster, Inc.
Produced by Cheshire Studio
Manufactured in the United States of America
First Edition
2 4 6 8 10 9 7 5 3 1
ISBN-13: 978-1-4169-0705-3
ISBN-10: 1-4169-0705-X

The mystery of the dinosaur in the forest began one fall day
when Freddie and Flossie, the younger Bobbsey twins, were
playing in their tree house.

Freddie and Flossie were pretending to be pirates sailing across the ocean in search of treasure. As Flossie took some beautiful jewels out of a wooden chest, Freddie scanned the horizon with his telescope, looking for ships.

"Wow!" Freddie said suddenly. "Look! It's . . . it's . . . a dinosaur! A real dinosaur!"

"I want to play *pirates*," said Flossie, "not pretend there are dinosaurs in the forest."

"I'm not pretending!" Freddie yelled as he peered through the telescope. He watched a giant, green dinosaur moving between the trees.

Flossie looked out the window but didn't see anything.

"Ooh! You missed it!" Freddie exclaimed, hurrying to the ladder. "Follow me. Maybe we can see it crossing the field."

The two Bobbseys scrambled down the ladder and set off to find the dinosaur.

"I still don't see anything," said Flossie as they approached the edge of the forest.

"The dinosaur must have been moving quickly," Freddie said.

"Look!" said Flossie, pointing to the ground. "Footprints!"

Sure enough, there was a trail of strange, circular footprints.

"Let's follow them," said Freddie. "They'll lead us to the dinosaur. I'm sure of it."

The twins followed the trail until it disappeared under a bunch of leaves. Feeling disappointed, they headed home.

"You couldn't have seen a dinosaur," Mrs. Bobbsey said after Freddie told her the story. "Dinosaurs died out millions of years ago."

"Maybe what you saw was a giant, green tree swaying in the wind," said Nan Bobbsey.

"But what about the footprints?" Freddie asked.

Nan's twin Bert shook his head. "From what you described, the footprints were too small to have been made by a big dinosaur."

"I *know* what I saw!" Freddie exclaimed. "Mom, can Flossie and I go see the professor? I bet he can help."

"You can go after lunch," said Mrs. Bobbsey.

An hour later, Freddie and Flossie went to see the professor. He wasn't a real professor, just a retired teacher who seemed to know everything about everything.

"Trying to solve another mystery, are you?" the professor asked as he leafed through a dusty old book. "Millions of years ago there were dinosaurs all over this area, but I'd be mighty surprised if . . ."

Just then the professor's wife appeared in the doorway, looking puzzled.

"Is something wrong, dear?" the professor asked.

"I'm sorry to interrupt," said the professor's wife, "but I can't seem to find the eye doctor's phone number."

"What for?" asked the professor.

"I think I need new glasses," his wife replied. "I was just driving by the high school and thought I saw a dinosaur."

Freddie and Flossie looked at each other with wide eyes.

"May I use your phone?" asked Freddie. "I need to call Bert and Nan and tell them to meet us at the high school right away!"

Freddie and Flossie said good-bye to the professor and ran as fast as they could toward the high school. Suddenly Flossie stopped in her tracks and gasped. She couldn't believe her eyes!

Looming over the high school was a huge, green dinosaur with big, sharp teeth!

Flossie turned to see if Freddie was as scared as she was, but her brother was grinning.

"What are you thinking?" Flossie asked.

"I'm thinking that we've solved the mystery of the dinosaur in the forest," said Freddie. "Follow me!"

"Wait up!" cried Flossie. "Why aren't you scared?"

"Because the dinosaur isn't real," said Freddie. "It's a balloon! There's a football game at the high school today."

Flossie burst out laughing, and Freddie joined in.
"Hey," said Freddie. "There's Nan and Bert. Let's all go see what's happening."

"I just talked to the visiting coach," said Bert a little while later. "His team is called the Dinos, and the balloon is their mascot. They carried the balloon all around Lakeport before the game to get people to come. It got us here!"

"But what about the footprints?" asked Flossie.

"They must have been made by the cleats the players were wearing," said Freddie.

"That's right," said Bert, putting his arm around his younger brother's shoulder. "It looks like you really did see a dinosaur in the forest after all!"